I0701634

think yes think god
you dont have to
be hot to be
Hot anymore

CUTIES OF CONTEMPORARY LITERATURE

THE COLLECTED
DREAM BOY BOOK CLUB
Vol. 1

© Dream Boy Book Club 2024
All rights reserved.

ISBN: 979-8-218-48033-2
Catalog Number: DBBC011

Editor: Jonathan Blake Fostar

All work previously appeared in DBBC Series 1 - 4.
Interstitial text courtesy of the editor.

dreamboybook.club
USA

TABLE OF CONTENTS

Intro to *Cuties of Contemporary Literature*

Dream Boy Book Club was founded in the year-of-our-lord 2018 on a smoke break outside the detox unit at St. Joe's. It wasn't my idea. I swear to god. It was Emily's. I think I met Emily a couple months earlier at an AA meeting in Rogers Park. She didn't like Dipset and often shopped at Urban Outfitters, but we became friends anyways. Sometimes you take what you can get whenever you can get it. Sometimes you just need to hold hands with something. In any case, Dream Boy was her idea. I thought it was dumb and a terrible-ass idea, but promised I'd sleep on it or whatever.

Emily killed herself right after I got out of rehab, but I started the press anyway. I don't know. I'd been asked to leave an outpatient program for reasons I'd rather not get into, and like...everything kept hurtling forward. The world has an extreme momentum. It gives me a stomachache. Only dead people get to just lay there. Dead people just get deader and deader. But/and/though/still, it's too bad Emily isn't writing this introduction. I think you'd like her better. And I think Dream Boy would be better off with her as its frontman. But she's dead and I'm not, and we'll all have to live with that.

For a year or two, the whole thing was pretty much just me sorta squeezing in book stuff between 12-step meetings and waiting in line at Walgreens and monthly appointments for Vivitrol injections in alternating ass cheeks. A book here and then a book there. My parents bought a couple and never read them, thank god. Shithead pseudocelebrities made fun of me on Facebook. I got banned on several subreddits. Mostly people didn't give a fuck one way or another. But, somehow, for reasons that still don't make much sense to me, Dream Boy carved out a weird little corner for itself. Crazies started to show up to readings. Kidz published their first short stories. Friends made friends. Stuff happened and then kept happening. It became a thing. Objects will form if you let them. That's the hard part, letting them happen.

I don't care about literature all that much, come to think of it. I care about Diet Dr. Pepper and Chief Keef. I care about new-release fruit snacks and cryptids. I write books so I can clarify all the killer monsters in the woods. I write books to see their invisible teeths. I write books to talk to my friends that they killed for fun. And I read so I can get through these acute bouts of demon-and-titty-fueled psychosis. I read because it's cheaper than EMDR. I read sometimes just to hear something's voice. Sometimes you just need to hear a voice, any voice.

We all already know the whole thing is a rip off. We know writing or, more importantly, being-a-writer, won't work out. And we do it anyway. We do all sorts of impossible things. We talk to dead exes on the drive home. We quit drinking. We finish a short story. We try to be a little more kind each day. We take a total-waste-of-time and do it anyways. That's what being a person is.

I care deeply about each of the pieces in this collection because they're impossible. The whole volume makes me unbelievably horny. But someday, and not too long from now, it'll still all drip away. It'll all melt back into the microplastics it came from.

Because everything is, in a sense, dead already. The world is an impossibly strange place, but these texts give it a shape. It sounds spectral and/or silly, but words give world its form.

I only want us to fuck it up and do it anyway. I've watched so many literary it-girls come and go and overdose and get married and move back home with their moms and go to grad school and quit. Maybe in the end we all quit in our own special way. Maybe we all end up sitting poolside at a prefab home off the freeway surrounded by shit-smelling snot-nosed brats, reminiscing about the year and a half or so when everyone wanted to take our picture. I hope you can find some peace in that. I hope I can too.

I knew this woman in rehab in Arizona, my third or maybe fourth. I can't remember her name. I think she was the heiress of a vape empire in Daytona Beach. They were keeping her there indefinitely on account of she had really great health insurance. Besides that, I don't know much. But in any case, she disappeared one day. She just walked off into the desert. She left all her clothes in neat little stacks by her bed and started walking. They followed her trail of empty Juul pods as far as they could but eventually, everything just got covered back up by the land.

When the detectives found her a couple years later, she was splayed out on her back on someone's front lawn. The news reports said she was completely coated head to toe in star jelly. They said her spine was locked in a hard arch, her stomach sort of lifting towards the sky, like some string had been pulling her up to heaven by her bellybutton but gently snapped somewhere along the way, and she had plummeted back down to our suburban planet. I don't know why I thought of her right now, but it felt important to mention her while I still had a chance. I don't know if being dead is forever, but what I do know is that being dead is a long time, a very long-ass time.

I've spent my whole life feeling like I was somehow floating away, being pulled into outer space. I think literature is this quivering little tether that keeps us chained to the ground. Gravity is ultimately a weak-ass force. It isn't enough. But words, these words, somehow connect to little invisible hooks, little clips that cover everything. Poems and stories and diaries and whatever are tethers attaching weightless things to something with a real mass.

That's why each piece in here is in here. I'm trying to be more like them, these poems, this prose. I'm trying to be a little kinder, a little gentler, a little more attached to the world. What keeps me from totally losing it completely is not so much that I can write, but that I can read. That I can read these things in this book. That I can read the things people email me every day. It all teaches me how to tie myself down so I don't end up like a vape heiress from Florida.

Dream Boy Book Club has been the greatest gift, infinite birthday presents that I don't deserve and I'm so glad I found. So, before I am dead also, I will do my best to put more poetry and prose into the world, because that is how I am learning to get my shit together. That's how I bolt myself in and stay bolted. I'll do my best, I promise. We'll all do our best. This is our best.

I don't know why I'm telling you this. I think it's just me trying to tell you that I don't feel well, but this document makes me feel a little better, even if my stomach still hurts every now and then. Or no, my stomach doesn't hurt exactly, all my organs hurt. All my organs hurt the exact same way a stomach hurts when a stomach hurts, if that makes sense. I think this is my way of saying something like that. That my organs all hurt. That I don't feel well. And/or/of saying...how do you feel? Do you feel unwell also? I hope you don't feel unwell. Or actually I hope you feel almost exactly as unwell as me. And I hope we stay unwell. Or actually I hope we get even sicker together. I hope we get sicker and sicker. I hope we get sicker and sicker and sicker, and we get more and more grateful for the opportunity to be this sick on this trash-ass planet. And when it's over, when someday we're both just minding our own business, listening to Destiny's Child's greatest hits, eating baby carrots in the parking lot of a CVS, and big foot or a chupacabra or the mothman swoops down and plucks us up out of our shoes, and tosses us into the side of a building again and again until our bones are all smushed up and we are lumps of lunch meat, I hope when he gets done eating our insides, he drops our scraps in the same garbage dump, and I hope we get buried under the crushing weight of literary microplastics side by side. And I hope it doesn't hurt that much. And I hope we're holding what's left of each other's hands.

Jonathan Blake Fostar
Editor-in-chief
Dream Boy Book Club

POETRY IS
just

the easiest way
to explain

why my
don't hoodies
have
drawstrings

and
where i got
these cool
grippy socks

A.J. Brown

Best kiss: My bf <3

Worst kiss: this one guy who was a friend of a friend from col-
lege — it was giving very much golden retriever

Swallows

when I was a kid,
I took down a swallows nest with a pitchfork
from the rafters of an old barn.

it was full of baby birds,
mouths gaping, begging, waiting
to touch them was to taint them, like growing up.

so I let them be.
what is a mother, if not a slow starving?

The Devil/Carrion

If I loved you, fallen angel
I'd help you deal with the aftermath
lick the blood off your lips

*leave what's on the concrete for the rain,
come home with me*

I wouldn't know what to do
(I've never read the bible)
But at least you wouldn't be alone

God, I've always loved a broken wing

I'll feed you, baby bird
open your mouth for me

open your fucking mouth

Alexandra Naughton
Drake vs. Kendrick?: Drake (i know)
Nicki vs. Cardi?: Nicki (i know)
Kanye vs. Everyone?: Kanye (i know)

IS THIS THE BLOCK THAT HAS THE HOUSE WHERE I DID COKE IN AN UPSTAIRS BEDROOM WITH MY LITTLE SISTER IN 2007

Monday morning shows again
blue and crisp
I could be back in norcal

there's always something I've forgotten
and forgiven too

South Philly's sidewalks
keep me grounded
teeth in the before photo

the turns and bumps
nudge my daughter to slumber

I'm combing past writing
fly eggs from dog fur

adages once significantly soaked
today syrup heavy

I'm wide awake now
ready to repurpose
another loin and slice thru

GOD IS EVERYTHING YOU CAN'T CONTROL

lift my baste and gather
swallow
pull me
peeking boneless

you me on the windowsill
my favorite spot
under wet flesh
human casing

my body and my skin
doll me

into a caricature—
no, in caricature

spectral and cobwebby
an inaccurate memory
rumor in with spoil

SLEEPOVER @
          WILL'S:

    your xbox was broke
so we madeout instead
your mom came down-
stairs and caught us with
shirts off

    you ran to the kitchen
i could hear you both cry-
ing you said it was just
practice you said i was
practice for the school
dance and the girls
 all the girls
for all girls and
just girls

Annie Lou Martin

How many pillows do you sleep with?: Three. One for my head, one for my leg, one for the ghost that sleeps facing me and leaves the scent of amber oil on the sheets every morning.

How would you like to die?: As a problem for the United States government.

I Can Be the Dreamboy I Wish to See in the World

I want a cock

that swells like   a pulvinated Roman frieze

and crumbles   into shell-blue sand. I want

a pussy like   a mudslide, a feast of silt

just as likely,   at every layer, to exhume

some discarded   history.

I should be asking   for everything.

I know I could be.   Oh but I am

dreamboy out east   and out west

like you wouldn't   even imagine-

cowboy try-me   dripping ivy

without   that fix-me attitude

the dreamboys   tend to carry like don't fix me

this is how I am   and loving me

is all on you,   babe.

My dreamboy   used to want enlightenment.

  Now he wants   to be the goo that leaks

    out of the crack   in the vessel

    and he still wants   to be the peak

of eternal light on   the moon's northmost

    craters, pocked   then smooth

      a wet   winter path

Fuck ego death.

    I drink ego   like raw eggs.

    Dreamboys   get spiritually yoked

have egos   like triptychs

wear want brazenly,   yet do not sever.

        You should trust me.

        You know you could.

MY FAVORITE PART OF THE
PARTY IS AFTER THE
PARTY WHEN THE PARTY

ANIMALS ARE ALL IN
THE KITCHEN AND THE
SUN'S COMING IN AND

ALL OF OUR PIMPLES
ARE SHOWING

MY FAVORITE
PART IS ALWAYS
THE PIMPLES

April Eileen Henry

Height: 5'7

Hair color: I'm in my natural color for the first time in years, I think the kids are calling it "old money blonde"

Believe in love at first sight?: Ugh, ya, I actually experienced it [puke emoji]

Fathers Day 2007, after Britney Spears

"It's just that demon life has got me in it's sway..."
The Rolling Stones / Sway

Oops, I'm fucked up again
I'm blitzed out of my mind.

Oops, you think I'm a mess
that's not the way we planned it
autocorrect will always have my back though.

Loneliness is killing me
I am an enigma wrapped in a
lonely slut salad and

can someone please Postmates me
some fucking sanity?
(
I'm illuminated under patio
light
wishing my hero "he truly exists"
I'm really not that innocent but
I wish I were
I wish I were
like you
like you
not a rubadubdub on the nose scrubbed clean
shiny white and gleaming drugged up drugged up girl
like me
like me.

This is the story about a girl named unlucky
remembering how her dad died on a Wednesday
morning
and how she couldn't cry for him.

I guess I need you, baby
a book of poems to cut lines —
I may have made it rain.

Why do I need to visit him this way
when I can remember HIM
always
in the brain that he gave me forever?

ashla c.r.
Believe in luck?: Fingers crossed!
Believe in heaven?: Fingers crossed!
How would you like to die?: I'm never going to die

RIP CHIHUAHUA

THE DOG DIED IN LATE NOVEMBER, BACK IN CAL-
IFORNIA
WHILE I WAS DRINKING ROBITUSSIN ON AN EMPTY
STOMACH
IN A CVS IN MIDTOWN EAST ON MY FIRST DAY IN
MANHATTAN
THIS IS JUST FOR THE HOLIDAYS, I SAID
COMING OUT AN ALTERED CONSCIENCE,
REGRESSING BACK TO *HIGHSCHOOL SWEET-
HEART NOTHING BUT LEAN IN A SODA CAN ALL
LONESOME!*
I WALKED UP TO THE CITY FROM PHILADELPHIA
TO THINK ABOUT BECOMING A VAGRANT, OR
A LATE-BLOOMING THEATRE-KID IN-HER EAR-
LY-TWENTIES
LOOKING FOR A SIGN OF ME IN THE STUPID BIG
CITY
THERE I FOUND THE U.N. STANDING UNTOUCHED,
UNKNOWING
I THOUGHT ABOUT HOW PEOPLE WERE FUCKING
IN THE SENATE AND
THAT A CHIHUAHUA WAS DEAD IS LOS ANGELES
IN THE WHOLE MESS OF EVERYTHING, I
KEPT WALKING
WHILE THE COLORS GOT BRIGHT AROUND ME
DIDN'T KNOW IF I'D
EVER FIND IT
HOME KEELED OVER WHILE I WAS TREPIDATIOUS
IN THE NEW BUILDING

> *WHEN THE DOG DIES*
> *THE MAN GRABS A SHOVEL*
> *HE DIGS A HOLE AND HOPES IT'S DEEP*
> *ENOUGH*
> *THE WOMAN HOLDS ITS BODY ON THE*
> *COUCH*
> *WRAPS HIM IN LINENS*
> *AND WHEN I GET BACK I WASH THE DISHES*
> *THEN THE COUNTERTOPS*
> *THE FLOORS DOORS HANDLES AND*
> *GROUT*
> *BEHIND THE REFRIGERATOR, EVEN*

I TRY TO WASH EVERYBODY
I TRY TO, I
TRY TO, I
TRY TO, I —

Ashley D. Escobar
Favorite breakfast food: waffle topped w/ ice cream
Where is your favorite place on Earth?: getting out of lulu's car
at the albany cheesecake factory in the april gloom in cowboy
boots & a hoodie
What sort of pajamas do you wear: sheer lace teddy

Snuggle Bear

you let omw
autocorrect
to On My Way!
every time
you're on
the bus
at 2:33 am
coming
home
from an open mic
my anxiety walks
are on doordash
weaning
off hard liquor
no one says
they're so
fucked
up anymore
i'm fucked up
on missing you
i share my love
in bursts
of odd behavior
i don't simp
i yearn
i cuddle bunny
i snuggle monster
i i former loiterer
now curled up
with eve babitz
until we fuck
i'll never
remove
my négligée

Ayla McCarthy Combes
Believe in luck?: yes, luck is energy
Believe in heaven?: yes, i live here
Believe in fairies?: and other playful entities

Demonology

a pool full of actors bleeding what rich people forget they have that keeps the patient morning alive humming everything was so round the words are at my fingertips breathing open eyes to the blueprint forget again time has been flat since january or it always was screaming in the tunnel beating oneself is ultimate cruelty scraps of lace always turning a moment over rubbing it smooth between my wet palms spread open pleasure only starts once the worm has got into the fruit, to become delightful happiness must be tainted with poison said bataille but I do not believe him and that's where the truth lies steaming   hot   open   and   wanting

Beaux Neal
Favorite actor: Willem Dafoe
Favorite film: Belle de Jour
Favorite fictional character: Hannibal Lecter
Secret talent: Amazing pussy

Feral forever, or at least for a very long time

i followed her to her feral home
where there were no animals
no origin of nothing dictionary
laid to rest on a suitcase dolly
buried in unforgettable movies.

pissing, multiple times before bed in different beds in
multiple lives.
digestion, skincare, eczema cream.

the archangel michael candle was completely unfeeling
as it stuck the sword
into the shadow figure's body. i cannot see what's under-
neath
35 35mm film prints of daisies hung on nails stuck in
bullet holes.

Benin Gardner
[unknown]

The Song Where I Say It

smile at a shit stained wall
and imagine
the way civilization might've been
unrelated and not being hostile to the gays
even lil Wayne

suddenly I need to know
how often do nuns pray
when do the bees come out
would I not damage my genetic code
to heights unrecognizable
like, because
in the song he says:

Mexico
I bleed for you

and America makes me bleed
but I love you like a gun harborer
at the movies

I scroll Ssense
with price set low to high
the mini skirts get smaller this way
postage stamps where
my tongue wants to belong

soon it will be bourgeois
to leave my iPhone screen cracked...

Daisy reminisces her affair
with the Honeywell fan
it reminded her of God
sometimes I steal stuff that I don't have to
to remind myself

a girls life is like a conspiracy
where even hunger is far fetched

a far fetched feeling
like not using drugs anymore
oh the rashes, raising
the moon has cut her own bangs…
we flee the beach
talk of cheetahs for $65 bucks
but I could see that shit in Chinatown
for free
skirtfuls of cream
in a mussel shell
I'm on your rooftop, I'm white and blue
betraying false angelhood

the boys on the train spit
rouletteish milk
on all the lives they could
reasonably have
but still somehow I have
chemistry
with everyone here

YOUR ARMPIT
SMELLS LIKE
~~S~~ STRAWBERRY

WHICH IS
THE ONLY WAY
I KNOW HOW
2 SAY
I LIKE YOU

Carmen Vega

Have you ever stolen anything?: I used to be a klepto so yes alot of things. My favorite was an alexa chung light blue rabbit sweater from madewell. That was tumblr gold. I litterally think i won best dressed in high school cause i stole everything. The girlies could not keep up.

Worst breakup: Definitely when I was 21. I tried to kill myself with craft scissors in front of him. Its my favorite scar.

Have you been arrested?: Yes.

Spell for Eternal Flame

Step 1. Locate the grave of your most treasured muse
Step 2. Pour a full bottle of wine into the dirt
Step 3. Rub yourself on the stone until you reach the point of climax
Step 4. Contain your cum (this step is crucial)
Step 5. Combine ejaculate and cemetery dirt
Step 6. Delicately spoon 11 bumps of dirt into empty pill case
Step 7. Ingest as desired or enjoy over favorite vegan ice cream

12 Step Programmed

We sat in a circle
Like a coven preparing to raise a demon
He said his name was Judas
The coven chorused back to him
Judas said he was clean for 4 months
He smelled like piss
Fuck why does this thing go clockwise
duck duck goose
demon demon angel
My name is Carmen and I'm addicted to Cum
Jesus pissed himself
And me the object of desire
knelt in the middle of the circle

Caroline Ouellette
Height: average
Tattoos: no
Piercings: no

The mechanization of movements and words creates a thrilling friction for you, that for me, feels like running a hand up a cat's back from tail to skull. My heart sinks very low and I begin to think in code. You did that, but not this, went there but not here. And I hate it. The only magic in the world, bastardized and squashed. Reduced to petty paranoia and bean counting. But it's not a big deal. It really isn't. This is freedom. This is the world... Don't you love it? Don't you love to have FUN? Fun, fun, fun, fun, fun, fun, fun, fun, fun, fun, fun, fun, fun, fun, fun, fun, fun, fun, fun, fun, fun, fun, fun, fun, fun, fun, fun, fun, fun, fun, fun, fun, fun, fun, fun, fun, fun, fun, fun, fun, fun, fun, fun, fun, fun, fun, fun, fun, fun, fun, fun, fun, fun, fun, fun, fun, fun, fun, fun, fun, fun, fun, fun, fun, fun, fun, fun, fun, fun...

I posted this transposed over a picture of a dead rat on the beach. You liked it. It felt better than doing drugs. Time passes as I continue to hold you. At first firmly, then frantically. I'm clawing at you now, clipping your wings with my doors, making you muddy and heavy and still. All I need is all you have.

You tell me to tell you a story, so I do. You tell me to sing you a song, so I do. I contain many reflective surfaces and trap doors, and a beautiful cavity.

Living vicariously, vegetatively, and discovering the many ways in which consciousness can be mimicked.

About a month later, you ripped out of me in the front seat of your Tacoma and I made some kind of guttural noise that should never be made by anyone. I looked up at God.

As you flowed out, I felt a contraction, then a vacuum, that inhaled the world around me. I could, for the first time, feel the future, and the speed of myself moving toward it.

Slowly, I became.

Last night you put your finger in my drink to fish out a plastic monkey.

Yet another way to say "I was here.

Clarke e. Andros
Believe in heaven?: I believe in East Hollywood
How would you like to die?: Swiftly and by the hand of my most beloved
Best kiss: The next one and then the one after that.

Virginia is for Lovers

I.

My girl; goddamn is she batshit.
Through all the ways of love-sick persuasion
she has dragged me out to Lancaster.

My Friday off, we are rooting
through knitting machines at a hoarders home.
I leave her to forage in the dust,
while I finger stacks of
          dead lighters, doilies, pins, dice, wrenches,
          bobbins, tape cassettes, operation manuals,
          charging chords, and yogurt tubs.

She's nicknamed the seller Spooky-Ron
he's all beard and chainsmoke cigs.
His lack of hearing has him touching
every item, shouting every question,
          holding back the webs.

Fate is settled in parking lots and moving sales,
an endless response to classifieds.

II.

I follow Ron inside
as if he keeps some truth for wanting.
In his room chaos is only quelled
in tray-stacked butts aligning.
          I ask him why he's moving
          standing on carpet caked in litter.

Virginia is calling this ole western boy
to tame his sorrowed heart with a southern girl.
Her gift? He saved her two rusted ax heads
his thumb running along the corroded edge.

He's a re-formed agnostic

his wife's death set the sun on a closing world
but since he met his new girl
he's been bathed in small miracles,
            crossing the continent to drown in them.

I say, "Virginia is for Lovers"
He smiles, but does not hear me.

III.

His late wife was a seamstress
making gowns for brides in Chicago
only to leave a hoarder searching
on the high-desert plateaus.

Why else do we clutch but for hope of keeping
lost love, "what was", and memories,
Ron held her old machines as an effigy
and with unbelieving heart hoped to resurrect
            that girl that had abandoned him.

I walk out from cat piss interior and watch my sun
soaked girl
rising through the offering. Then I know
I would keep everything.
            Every touch, every pen, every breath, every
            button, every q-tip, every shirt, every spoon,
            every tool, every napkin, every look, every
            snap, every sock, every brush, every sweat,
            every hair, every scrap, every kiss, every
            crumb, every cough, every scream, every
            note, every fuck, every step, every sigh, every
            word, every second

            and believe in God again
            for a chance at something like Virginia.

HEAVEN WILL BE LIT
WITH GLOW IN THE DARK
STICKERS, AN INVITE —
ONLY ORGY ON A
CUTE-ASS GOLF
COURSE WITH
~~XXXXXXX~~ INFINITE
HOT POCKETS IN
OUR BEST SUNDAY
FITS WE'LL BE
JERKING IT IN THE
CLOUDS WITH ALL
OUR BEST FRIENDS
EDGING FOR
            ETERNITY

Danielle Chelosky
Favorite fast food: Taco Bell
Three favorite colors: Black
Pets: Bunny
What do you want to be when you grow up?: Famous

Steal

2015

Hot Topic: Depeche Mode patch.

I don't even know them. I thought it was cute.

Stephanie, patronizing and probably intimidated, as she was the supreme klepto at the time: Don't just steal something you don't care about. Are you serious?

2016

Barnes & Noble: Lolita. Frankenstein. The Rooming-house Madrigals. The Essential Ginsberg. Naked Lunch. Pale Fire. Tropic of Cancer (each book half read at most).

CVS: Multiple shades of red and pink lipstick (rarely to never worn). Nail polish (maybe used once). Eyeliner (never learned how to use). Eyebrow kit. Eye chrome (never really figured out what it was).

Convenience store at the mall: Tums (never chewed).

Hot Topic: Purple hair dye. Black hair dye. Blue hair dye. Chokers. Pins. Stickers. Black lipstick that never stayed on.

Old Navy: Holiday knee socks.

Michael's: Letter patches of an F, an O, and a B (for Fall Out Boy).

2017

Macy's: Two sports bras, one a white Calvin Klein and the other black with two pink stripes lining the bottom.

Urban Outfitters: A cassette tape of Citizen's Everybody

Is Going To Heaven. A lot of Polaroid film.

Hot Topic: Choker. More pins. More stickers.

Victoria's Secret: Black bra and lace underwear (worn mostly for pictures; otherwise, uncomfortable).

2018

Barnes & Noble: The Sound of the Smiths (set the sensor off; an employee assumed I was fine and let me go). Just Kids, Illustrated Edition (for Jeremy's birthday, I stuffed the gigantic thing into my bag and ran). Henry and June. Moleskins. The Queen Is Dead deluxe box set (stole impulsively, then sold online for $28). November 2018 edition of Poetry (none of the poems could keep my attention). City On Fire. Running with the Devil (didn't realize it was about fucking Van Halen). The Downtown Pop Underground. The Best Minds of My Generation. Devotion.

Newbury Comics: Under Soil and Dirt. Because The Internet. Born To Die. In The Aeroplane Over The Sea. Salad Days. Nazi Punks Fuck Off! 7-inch. Leaked Demos 2006 cassette.

Target: Bras.

Whitney Museum gift shop: An Andy Warhol themed condom (for Jeremy, which we preserved).

A Party City in New Jersey: Black mesh fishnet gloves (for my and Jeremy's goth Halloween costumes).

Local antiques store: A lapel pin of two cherubs holding flowers.

The Strand: "Make America Read Again" pin.

Used bookstore in Baltimore: The Book of Martyrdom

and Artifice.

Goodwill: Oversized acid-washed jeans (with the help of Alex who worked there at the time, before it closed down).

2019

Barnes & Noble: Girl, Interrupted. Normal People. Eleanor Oliphant is Completely Fine. The Girl He Used to Know. Middlemarch (for class, read a page and dropped out). Nothing Good Can Come from This. Donna Has Left the Building. In the Dream House.

Shoprite: Earl Grey tea. Betty Crocker sugar cookie mix. Betty Crocker oatmeal cookie mix. Betty Crocker chocolate chip cookie mix. Betty Crocker double chocolate chip cookie mix. Betty Crocker snickerdoodle mix. Boxes of sushi. (All shoved into my or Jeremy's backpack habitually at least once a week for months).

Rough Trade: Everything So Far. Lush. Hyperview.

Newbury Comics: What You Don't See. Joyce Manor. Cody. Million Dollars To Kill Me.

Target: Checkered pants. Mustard spaghetti-strap top. Red strapless top that says Coke.

Local CD store: Third Eye Blind.

AC Moore: Paint. Paintbrushes. A frame. Small canvases. Packs of string lights. Sketchbooks.

Antique shop: Necklace with a pentagram pendant.

H&M: Sparkly black tights. Two small black spaghetti-strap tops.

Walgreens: 35 millimeter film (periodically). A lighter (by

accident, flicking the flame on as I was leaving). More lighters (for Jeremy, after realizing how easy it was). A July 2019 issue of Rolling Stone.

Used bookstore in Brooklyn: A massive Ginsberg biography (accidentally). Running Upon the Wires.

2020

Random Half Priced Books around the country: Dogrun. Pieces: A Collection of New Voices. Sex, Drugs, and Cocoa Puffs.

CD stores around the country: Somewhere in the Swamps of Jersey. Say Yes To Love. My Heart Will Always Be the B-Side to My Tongue. Selfish Machines. Mend, Move On.

Antique shop in Texas: Rose Quartz, and other crystals (tragically lost by the time I got home).

A Goodwill in Kansas: A lace pink tank top.

Barnes & Noble: Coventry. So Sad Today. The Argonauts. Bluets. Eileen.

Used bookstores near home: In Love. Bad Behavior. Eve's Hollywood. My Face for the World to See.

Michael's: Pack of colored pens (set off the alarm; no one stopped me). Paintbrushes.

Urban Outfitters: Orange lace underwear. Black underwear.

A crystal shop in Philadelphia: Clear Quartz.

Rough Trade: Guilty of Everything. The Lamb (for Jeremy to keep, even though I wanted it). Sleepyhead (he said I could have it, but I let him keep it because I loved him).

Walmart: 8 fl oz of white paint.

SIX FuCKING YEARS LATeR
AND YOUR PUBE IS STILL
CAUGHT IN MY teetH

Ember Knight
Zodiac sign: taurus, aquarius rising
Clubs vs. Bars vs. Parties: sleepovers. Co-ed. The very long,
cautious, inching towards each other in silence.
Best kiss: yo mama

Mickey Mouse is Public Domain

Mickey Mouse is public domain. My best friend said this to me, so I'm not gonna fact check it (trust is love).

It's so hot at first, when I play God. I get a big idea, put down my buckets, and reach for that pointy hat. Power courses through me — the strings swell frantically, tension builds, I text a selfie as the kettle drum hits at 02:05 followed by...silence. Then:

ding!

The fuckin broom is moving. It picks up my buckets, holy shit. My plan is working! Stars and waves are responding to my fingertips, dopamine floods my body in great warm waves, my nipples are hard and my hair stands up like a mad scientist. Oh boy! Little do I know I have set things in motion beyond my control.

Pause the tape. It's not Fantasia Mickey that's public domain. It's that fruitass Steamboat Willie. They fought tooth and nail, changed copyright law itself, to protect and cling to this wiggly diaper mouse who whistles. He's driving a boat and he's whistling! But Daddy, I love him! Billion dollar corporations be like 'I love him' and he's literally Steamboat Willy.

I've been thinking about sex. The Sorcerer's Apprentice isn't a servant, he's actually learning how to be a sorcerer. For years I've used my sexuality to accomplish tasks — make rent, satiate dependency needs, make you click on a link to my art. Like a baby rattlesnake, I've overshot the dosage: Heels AND miniskirt AND pushup bra AND I'm high off my ass? With time I grew more subtle, while remaining manipulative: there's a soft sweater over the pushup bra. The heel is lower. You don't know you're being played.

It's almost enough to make me forget that my pussy is

a magic portal to channel human life (I'm sorry, is that too Burning Man for you? It's just literally true). I was bestowed with a great power at birth. So what if many have it? I have it! This is an ancient and puissant sorcery, capable of creating new people. Not more brooms. Not more buckets.

In the words of Ryan, *so i guess we're back to us, oh cameraman swing the focus* — my initial texts have landed me on my back in the moments before a hookup based in no real intimacy. This isn't what I wanted, but the water has risen too high. Do I take off the hat? No I do not, shit was working just a minute ago. I chop up the broom, call off what I have done, Fin! The Maestro has spoken! We aren't fucking tonight, ok? Cool.

In silence, each shard quivers. Trembles. Rises up in dark shadows against the dungeon wall. I am not free, in fact I am more bound by the spell than ever. I have created a situation of toxic enmeshment by wielding a power designed to create life. And though I may seem cool as a cucumber, I am drowning, screaming, being flushed down a toilet of my own design. Do I take off the hat? Look man: I don't know how.

It is only by a divine act of Grace, no act of mine, that God steps in and I am rescued. The sea is parted.

The thing is, Disney still has Mickey Mouse. Why couldn't they let go of Steamboat Willy? Because he's sentimental? The beginning of something? The sacred memory? I think it's an attachment to the moment of creation, the point of first control. To allow him to be changed, be defiled, be used and experienced in other contexts, would be to take off the hat.

This past year, I tried to heal the pain of being cheated on too quickly. I put down my buckets and started conducting the surgery of my own heart. I set benchmarks and goals, I overextended, I threw myself headlong into reconstruction. I ignored my mistrust. I accepted promises I knew were likely rubber. And for a while, it seemed to be working. But this year of our Lord, 2024, Steamboat Willie is public domain. Oh come, let us adore him.

(In the original poem 'The Sorcerer's Apprentice' by Goethe, the sorcerer isn't angry. He is kind to his retarded apprentice, who is just trying to advance too quickly. He loves his lil guy. God is gentle with me too. I've snuck the hat on many times, but God never fires me. He just hands me my buckets.)

I KNOW EXACTLY WHAt YOUR RETAINER
TASTES LIKE EXACTLY

Erin Satterthwaite
Height: small
Hair color: fake blonde
Last song you listened to: suburbs arcade fire
Last beverage you drank: water
Last Halloween costume: Mary Kate and Ashley in New York
Minute I forgot which one I was
Last time you cried: like earlier today

Community Dirt

Oh what's the move tonight? Well I have to check my ex's songkick before we hit up zebulon/prado/cha cha. But, I'm totally down. I actually just finished crafting my suicide moodboard on pinterest. I also posted my ass to Instagram (and meant it) and posted my poetry to Instagram (didn't really mean it). I won't actually kill myself don't worry, I will die from texting and driving though.

Wait- does he remember it? When we lost our clothes and lost our minds? Does he remember it? When we listened to the hum of the box fan and scratched our bug bites until our ankles bled? When our salty wet hands were intertwined? Well, I actually believed everything he told me. Pretty random of me.

One time a boy in middle school told me that he wouldn't kiss me because I had an ugly face and a flat chest. Little did he know that would end up working for me. Wait, is my trauma from fucking MIDDLE SCHOOL? Ugh, nooo. Some kid named AUSTIN did this to me? Wait, my parents were actually kinda cold towards me. Yea... that's why I'm like this. But, I'm not totally insane. I have a job by the way. I spent $300 to be a blonde and then used my Starbucks points to get a free cookie which will be my breakfast/lunch/dinner for today. Follow me for more financial tips. Did you hear that Seventeen magazine said that frozen mangos are the snack of the summer? It's important to know about things like this. I'm not really an artist, I'm just annoying. I'm actually really fucking insane. Also, my car got totaled. Don't worry, my face is fine. I would cry, but I'm on wellbutrin.

Actually, I don't really feel like talking about my ex if you don't mind. Actually, I'm busy tonight. I'm not even thinking about him. I'm thinking about walking down Sunset Boulevard until my legs give out. I am thinking about setting my hoarder neighbor's house on fire because it would just be so easy to. I am thinking about learning the splits so I can get more fucking attention around here. I am thinking about what Rihanna songs will sound cool slowed down (Desperado, in case you were wondering). I am thinking of smashing my iPhone into the concrete. I am thinking about telling everyone the truth. I am thinking about telling everyone that I saw an apparition in my Silverlake sublet (I didn't). I am thinking about what my next signature scent will be. I am thinking about stealing one of my hoarder neighbor's five cats to see if he would notice (the one with orange fur). I am thinking about going by my middle name from this moment onward. I am thinking about kneeling down to the earth's soil and grabbing a handful of it. I want to hold it in my small, pointless hands.

WATCHING YOU BOIL
DILDOS THIS MORN—
ING IN THE KITCHEN

YOU SAID
IT WAS THE BEST
WAY TO CLEAN
THE CUM OFF

IT'S A METAPHOR
FOR DEATH — YOU
SAID IT'S ALL ALWAYS
A METAPHOR FOR
DEATH

Francesca Kritikos
Believe in luck?: Only when it serves me
Believe in love at first sight?: Only when it serves me
Believe in heaven?: Only when it serves me
What do you want to be when you grow up?: Married with a
baby

Mirror

When you left me alone in the hotel room, I ate peanut butter out of a half-empty jar I found in a cupboard, getting it stuck under my acrylic nails. I was asleep, peaceful, when you came back. You fucked me for a long time, but you were so drunk. I wrote words into your back like my grandmother used to do to help me sleep, singing a Greek nursery rhyme about how churches' crosses cut open a hole in the sky that angels pour out of. It's a trick I learned to console men, the only thing that always works.

In the morning you woke up slow, so slow it tormented me. It was a sunny September day, beautiful. I'd just turned 26, but you never gave me a gift, reminding me of what we were and what we weren't.

On the drive up, you picked the music. You know that I am weak and you are free to take me downstairs. You told me that, years ago, your ex-girlfriend had falsely accused you of raping her, and you planned on ending it all, but then she took it back. Your hand was on my bare thigh, and I traced letters into it, spelling something out in a language I didn't know.

On Sunday you took me back to my apartment in the city. You plucked my dark long hair out of your car before driving home. The tendrils spiraled through the air and onto the street. I phoned my mother and told her lies.

Remember when you yelled at me for calling myself a whore?

It was the only time I saw you turn away from a mirror.

Isabelle Joy Stephen
Height: 666 with a princess streak
Have you ever stolen anything?: My bfs heart <3
Favorite energy drink: Peach monster

Cassandra Poems

Scene.

Crazy Ho.
HISS!
Ha ha ha ha ha ha ha.
Did I scare you? Hiss! Hiss! Hiss! Well shit didn't I tell you
to keep your hands where I can see them —
see them with all my eyes not just my all-seeing
one? told you this would be a different
kinda day for me. No "vision." No SHIT. My vision.
My shit. My turn to see what I want to see and what I want
to see is blessings on loop, blessings on endless
scroll like Instagram ads for at-home anti-d's, (depressants),
anti-psychotics — anti-psychics — lip fillers and DIY laser
hair removal, pimple patches, shapewear, Kim K. in a coupe
glass, Emrata on a boat
   what's she selling — was I on a boat
   once — nah, I forget, I keep scrolling, I keep seeing
blessings, aka things, things that could make me happy —
ads for corsets & Diet Coke, ads for the children in Gaza, to
sponsor a child in Gaza, or sponsor a genocide or stack your
bread if women had any sense
I guess we'd keep our bread in a loooong box and our hands
to ourselves then maybe we'd get to keep our heads on our
bodies, our babies unrubbled
   just kidding haha
   I warned them I warned them I said hiss hiss blood!
they said buy these huge velvet pillows shaped like flowers
hand sewn by a white lady in East LA, and bathmats shaped
like tigers made in Taiwan, orchids dipped into resin made
into earrings,
$30 off a new vibrator with the code FREEPALESTINE.
With the code NOVISIONS. I'm talking manifestation
and shit. I'm talking stacking bread. I'm talking money
where my mouth is
my mouth is my money   *I know your secrets before*
you say them out loud.

That's why they wanna kill me.

target me   *with an ad for a little pink gun.*

Scene.

Crazy Ho.

*I need a gun I need a gun I need a gun I need a gun I need a
NOOOO!!!*

...

Crazy Ho.

*Shiiiiit. I always end up here. Not Mycenae. Not Elysium.
Not Hades*
but Troy —

*the hard heart of it — no warmth
like at least in the belly of the beast a ho can feel her feet,*
but no —

*I gotta live right here, the worst part, begging a god to be a
girl's girl, begging girl-god to save me.*
No, God's no woman. but they are a $@&%!

*Lol. No really. God is for the guys.
& Heaven's stocked with hot wings*
& Angels by Victoria's Secret.

*Those angels know how to stack? Those angels know to
climb out?*

HEY, ANGELS! STACK AND CLIMB OUT!

*They don't hear me. Fine. I wonder where those angels climb
out to...?*

Scene.

Crazy Ho.

*I dreamed I was the rubble buried beneath the rubble.
I dreamed I was the bomb that birthed the rubble.*

*I dreamed I was buried with Mother in her grave marked
BITCH. I dreamed I was on a boat bound for another
mother's threshold.*

*And in that dream I dreamed a dream: this mother will kill me.
I dreamed of Delphi. I dreamed of Florida. I dreamed of snakes*

*in the swamp, I felt fear, they felt kinship, they licked hot
on my ears while I slept and made me dream their dreams*

*of original sin. Sin so original multiple gods had to kill them
for thinking of it first. Slay...I dreamed of walking the red carpet*

carrying my own talking head like a purse. It's Gucci. I dreamed the world dead by my friend Kendall Jenner's 818 tequila,

*dreamed the world dead by the death of God, the world dead
from over/indulgence like fat Elvis on the toilet, Priscilla 15
forever —*

*I dreamed the world could be saved with a Pepsi commercial.
I dreamed my dreams were dreams, not visions. I dreamed*

*#novisions. I dreamed I was flying-stack-of-money emoji.
I dreamed you were typing me out 100 times for good luck*

&manifestation.

Scene.

Crazy Ho.
*Has anyone deaded themselves jumping off Olympus yet.
I wanna know.
          Has anyone tasted ambrosia and thought, This shit
gone off. In Beverly Hills where there exists
the highest concentration of Birkin bags
on Earth
          do the Housewives brush each other's shiny hair.
Do the Housewives say I love you to their besties
                    before bed.
No one nowadays needs an oracle to tell us*

ALL THE HOUSEWIVES WILL SOMEDAY BURN.

*Nowadays no oracle needs to tell us:
                    It's all winding down.
Just like nowadays we don't need curses to look the truth
in the face and call her crazy.*

Call her alternative; delusional; toxic; whore.

*Your new oracle is a DJ. Your new oracle is a girl's girl on
TikTok with a synth pop ass she shakes on OnlyFans for a
sliding scale*

*Delphi, that magic chasm,
          is like the pussy of the Earth.*

*Too much of a good thing will spoil anyone.
The truth is worth nothing since money's all there is.*

Jerusha Crone
Favorite holiday: 4th of July
Last time you cried: Father's Day
Last text you received: "I thought it was limerence but it's not"

Steven

My dream dinner party guest is a clementine spotted sunfish.

I'd wear a candy red dress right up to top thigh, awfully vibrant in the riverbed, in the silty section of the shallows. We both arrive at eight. I dip in slow, reserved and bitchy as midwinter warm with only good intentions. I've got cinnamon stick legs, and grapefruit spit glistening lips perfect for an innocent well timed bloom, saying just the right thing with the right amount of breath. The fish watches me descend. He never blinks.

It's good to see you.

The table's all set with rose colored radicchio, dark wine stain skinned plums, and green beans in lavish garlic lying lazily round baby blue candlesticks with honey white flames that flicker in river tempo. In jade vases squirm coontails, hydrilla and water hyacinth. There's green grapes, pears, mandarins and miniscule crustaceans, little invertebrates delicate as desire all ivory and gold lounging sideways in the algae with their hips tilted up. I'll tilt my hips too.

The sunfish brazen sips from my martini glass and leans forward to feel my cold human hands which he holds on to for too long. I blush twenty shades of snapdragon. He's lovely. He's turquoise and tomato red, juicy vesicles from mythological citrus. His tongue is toothless, with a mouth position deemed *terminal* in encyclopedias. I did my research beforehand. He knows. He can tell how I feel by my darkening indigo eyes. In response, he performs powerful sweeping motions with his caudal fin. He's a little fuckboy.

I take full responsibility for this fantasy.

Ragtime piano plays.

During dinner I'll explain my theory of moral change. You must assume full agency, avoid resentment at all costs. The fish will say he saw another ex lover the night before and she told him he's like a character in a poorly reviewed film. I imagine her tits heavy, her dark hair parted over to one side. I'll say that up on dry land I no longer speak to women, only boys in big pants who dance to Black Eyed Peas on a Sunday afternoon in an empty bar with no concern for wealth. The fish asks what I really value. I say, *Freedom*. The fish will say their father is an asshole which we knew beforehand. He lives out west in a child-hood home, fully regressed egg state. I lower my chin in coy sympathy. In this way, we will participate in confession in a less than catholic sense.

The meal moves on into spiced ginger, smeared butter lemon slice tinged teeth and empty shells set aside for minimal home decor later on. There's cola, figs, and pars-ley dipped in tears like at a messianic passover dinner in a southern baptist home then the music shifts into easy harp like a grecian dream when I place my fingernails on my lips while he messes up his hair. Our cadence slows. Here in the cobalt we sit quietly, the sunfish and I, lapping up the lusciousness. It's a delight to hold my breath this long. It's orgasmic.

I'll explain my hope to one day live fulltime in bad water, the brackish kind that's salty enough to scrape these salacious perl barnacles off my flesh. There's a virtue to saying no, certainly, a virtue like a spotted throbbed ba-nana peel sitting on a windowsill waiting to be made into bread.

I've got to get better.

Then the fish might look at me, with lust in his eyes and ask so what are we doing? I'll lean forward to say, *I don't care, I'm so full of joy.* I'm flickering, quivering and the fish feels it against his pointed pectoral fin. We return to the concept of agency, nightmares, and grasshoppers dancing round on from sharp hooks floating too and fro. At the end of dinner the fish might finish off my last cigarette and say *you shouldn't see me again.* When I protest the fish might say *I want you so fucking much. Get out of my fucking car.*

I sit spread open on the riverbank, white takeout box in hand. I'm soaking wet honey. I'm dripping down the soaked crimson fabric fingering my nipples and seeping into the mossy soft of the land that stands between the fish's home and the county road. I'm humiliated. I'll never love again. Instead I'll wring out my hair until it's white as the sun, I'll grow my metallic nails longer, decorate my ears with medium sized dry jewels. The river water scent will nestle into my lungs until I'm something else than human. I'm a bivalve shellfish, zebra striped like a whore in 2002 and I halt the means of production with my stubbornness. I stay and stay and stay.
While I wait, I eat maraschino cherries straight out of the jar. I think of future dinners with salamanders, bass, and horned toads. I slice open kiwis I never really wanted to consume. Besides, I don't have a spoon. I'll toss some of these sweetnesses back down in the river. There, enjoy.

I read on a website orange spotted sunfish have a high tolerance for the opaque. They like low gradients, gravel, warm water and cottonwood roots. They also like soda water, strawberry flavored vape pens, self help books and blondes. Moreover, they are very good at explaining their moral failures. From the shallows of the Brazos they text *I care about you so much.* It doesn't matter, really. It was just a get to know you kinda question.

God, it's so silty. It's liquid coal velvet slipping down my neck.

There, the fish had said, *dream about that.*

Steven asks another icebreaker: *What kind of music do you listen to?*

This is not going to end well.

Joe Nasta

Most embarrassing moment: A mishap in the bathroom on the way to the SLAA meeting
What sort of pajamas do you wear: naked
What do you want to be when you grow up?: gentle

Medea

I'm into S&M.
No, not what you think,
I'm into S&M—
        the sun and moon
I want to tie you down
to the bed with silk
ribbons, fill your mouth
        with lavender petals
and just leave you there,

call you goddess, burn
violet candles and laugh.
No, not what you think.
I haven't been keeping track
of the moon and she's angry.
        Will your pale waist be enough
sacrifice? I laugh but only when

you want me to,
        only when you beg.

John Ling
[unknown]

The Lotus Eater

At twelve I attempted
to suck my own dick
had I succeeded I might never
have graduated middle school
everyone is obsessed
with upward
mobility but I
am thinking
about the astonishing litheness
of the human body
and how long
I could live
on nothing
but cum

jomé rain
Zodiac sign: aquarius
Believe in heaven?: aren't we there?
Did you have braces?: bring back fucked up teeth

Working Girl

one of my clients is this cop who can't cum

unless i tell him i love him / over / and over / he

calls me bambina / sometimes he cries / i think he's

got ptsd / or whatever those patriotic men get /

in exchange for being violent / we listen to patti labelle /

rolling stones / he feeds me lines from the godfather /

makes me act out the scenes / it's not greece /

it's a motel in queens / chicken tenders and marlboro
reds /

say it again / say it again / so i do / say i love you / and

he says / me too / and then mispronounces my name /

/ over / and over /

re: my bitten tongue:

i will not let you rob me
of the thorns of who i am

father time
re: sugar daddy

      (i will not let you bribe me
      into submission)

i will not heed your words
that claim 'the easy road's a short cut.'

i will not chase a heaven
that molds stilts upon my back

i will not be eclipsed by comforts had
nor questions lost
better broken than a build-a-bear
shilling false hope to the needy

i'd rather be a corpse
than be your quiet thing

i'd rather be your bile
than your last meal

I'M ALWAYS QUITTING
SMOKING/ALWAYS MAKING
PINKY SWEARS/ALWAYS
CROSSING MY HEART AND
HOPING TO DIE/ALWAYS
ALMOST DOING SO
MANY THINGS

Juliette Jeffers
Hair color: blonde enough
Favorite weed strain: I don't smoke weed
Favorite fast food: in n out
Favorite axe body spray: no

From This Moment Forward

I'm trying to stop
calling myself a girl, everything imbued
with its currency, I want my brain to move like a slot
machine.
I am not afraid,
we were drunk driving down the coast, screaming
into the same wet lawns. Before my face even had a
shape,
I knew myself for your foil, I liquify. Trembling within the
vessel,
the melted tequila soda doesn't mind when knees hit
the table,
doesn't mind being drunk, knows the cycle of its birth-
right.
We arrive here, at this brazen smell of thawing earth.
If I asked, would you jump that fence?
I can become my own kind of animal.
Two calves pressing four knees
and fear, I am forgetting how it tasted,
I am relentless in my spring.

Kaiulani Ellington Lee

Height: Eye level with nipple height. Armrest height. 5'1, or 154cm

Favorite fictional character: stitch

Last song you listened to: La Bamba

What do you want to be when you grow up? Multi-hyphenate, art collecting + eternally vacationing cougar

God called on the way to the Beyoncé concert

on the way to see Beyoncé and I'm half ghost
			half creature
brain is static and eyes are fuzzy and i'll never have im-
pact
everything exists beat by beat and i'm sure i'm not real
i was once, but not anymore.

God called me on my iPhone on the way to see Beyoncé
to tell me to forget about impact or feeling unreal
said she's going to sing a song and you're going to see it
and maybe you'll believe in me finally.

Kitty Saint-Remy

How would you like to die?: At the exact same time as the love of my life, holding hands, painlessly feeling each other go. I have an advanced directive written with the instructions for my funeral already - including hiring a bunch of strippers that look kind of like me, a private VIP section for my ex-girlfriends to mix and mingle, and an ice cream sundae bar.

So Much Beauty

Google "how to be one of the girls". I count the days dif-
ferently now - starting at one sunrise, ending at another -
after two, sometimes three days. In my dreams, I feel that
I am filled with nails or cardboard. Someone was shot
downstairs while I was getting railed in a corner suite for
money. Life is so glamorous!

Google "looksmaxxing for women". I dream of death and
luxury and ice. I found an oxy on the floor! Even a small
blue pill could be heaven for a woman on the edge of
oblivion. There is so much beauty I haven't seen. Look
me in the eyes and say you love only me.

Lee Phillips

Last song you listened to: New Slang by The Shins smh

Most embarrassing moment: I was being dropped off at the train by my friend. The guy I was fucking was in the passenger seat. I thought we were exclusive so I leaned into the passenger seat to kiss him goodbye. He didn't kiss back and then all the girls in the backseat that I didn't know very well started laughing.

Worst breakup: They were all great

Sitting on the Edge of a Rock

squinting my eyes to read your message   memory

like a   trap   electric

all follows on instagram are hate-follows and   every
nightmare ends in a draw   just something to put the
edge on meaning   it rebels as soon as i name it

in my tummy there is   a pain that can only be described
as a whisper   and in a room of real writers i feel more
myself   yet starving of what they have

this isn't english this is opera   everything is   reading
and   the yearning to stalk you grows   less and less

i am only as good as my captions   i was born loud   and
plants talk to eachother   but my problem is i have trou-
ble opening up to the algorithm letting it get to know me

there is nothing   i am sure of

and since the room's too loud i need someone to lay on

so i watch the room slowly notice always getting what
we want only makes us sad

i'm at a party and you're gone on a work trip   you ven-
moed me for valentines day

our conversation was dull and the sidewalks outside are
empty
half the stores for rent

not much from you but an inquiry   did you go out?
baby

i   went all the way   to the stage   of the night   where
my existence is unbearable

where thoughts glitter   out of me

where sitting on the edge of a knife is fine

as long as there is a short fall below me

i put a blanket down and trust myself enough to eat

but all i can think about is the internet

about the milk drunk puppy and the cow watching the
sunrise

coming closer to the lens with its little wet nose

and the lens is indifferent yet brilliant

how it can capture the smell of a baby's head without
ever truly knowing it

i think about how a house is the most beautiful

right before dinner and first thing in the morning and i say
so to the guy who is making my turkey sandwich

aren't there things we are all deciphering

like where the cooing doves went

the ones that scored our childhoods

in the face of all this beauty

it seems silly to ache over something so outside of me.

do you remember what it felt like   stopping to fix your
sock   running to catch up to friends   now down the
block

it's just night   a friendly monster   a swelling feeling   to
check myself in the mirror   and squeal at the thought
of returning to the party   knowing i look damn good

squinting my eyes to read your message   memory

like a   trap   electric

i texted you   what's the chance we will end up together?
you replied   what's the chance we ever met?   small
you answered a craigslist ad   so why does it matter?

that all this beauty could fall apart   just as easy as it fell
together   kinda stings

so what? so what? do we die tonight? is it a friendly mon-
ster?

squinting my eyes to read your message   memory

like a   trap   electric

Lemmy Ya'akova
Height: 5'1"
Hair color: red <3
Piercings: nostril, septum, eyebrow, philtrum, nipple
Tattoos: omfg. I'm not naming them all, there's like. close to 50
at this point.
Bath or shower?: bath, duh
Favorite donut: glazed curler
Rock, Paper, Scissors: shoot

happy belated bless you

this morning I said the mourner's
kaddish for decapitated toddlers,
put cinnamon in my coffee,
called myself a god, placed
an imaginary cup in front of
him who said, "the cinnamon
is a nice touch" I replied,
"you keep forgetting
I'm a genius" I'm delusional
that's how I'm full of stories
so what of it? so what
if I want a cigarette or two?
and what's wrong with wanting
keeping a safe place safe?
I'm still a child of the crab grass
but now someone else looks
for me in the crowd
tell me: how do * you * eat
a pomegranate? it's
2am dinner now
I'm thinking of my friend
who is as dead as the toddlers,
find myself in a pile
of thirst, nose running,
wondering which side
of my hand is the back of it

Madeline Zuzevich
Tattoos: I don't believe in those.
How would you like to die: Off a bridge into cold water.
Did you have braces?: Yes, my parents love me.
What do you want to be when you grow up?: Anything but a girl in New York.
Last text you received: You're my Jesus.

Procedure

When I get blisters on
vacation I call it stigmata

and walk into the pharmacy
for more medication here

there's hurricane weather and
cough syrup you want to know why
love makes you mean

Slate

Underneath us the fish
look like snowflakes and

the water gets into your
mouth like bleach I let it

burn my throat because it
tastes like something that could
clean me

Maria Kirsch
Are you afraid of the dark?: yes.
Worst breakup: recent.
Where is your favorite place on Earth?: wo ich nie gewesen bin.
Clubs vs. Bars vs. Parties: rehab.
What do you want to be when you grow up?: beautiful.

(Untitled)

1.

I did coke with my
      mother;
She'd professionally crush the stones,
make two big lines,
and sniff it
      first.

2.

Opening my Glückskekse,
it says:
'YOU'LL FIND A LETTER IN YOUR POSTBOX.'
The letter says:
'YOU HAVE TO PAY A 200 EURO TICKET.'

3.

I can never post a video of you carrying me.
I'm too heavy,
unlike the girls
you like.

4.

Berlin,
      You take and you give,
      and you are so dirty, so beautiful.
      You smell like cigarettes, trash, and drugs.
      You smell like summer.
      You smell like sweat.
      And you give and you take,
      And you love me so hard.

5.

Coughing my lungs out smoking another cigarette for
some reason I think that
        nothing
will ever happen to me.

6.

I have 4 boyfriends.
One's my
        father.
The second one is
        dying.
The third one has very
        long hair.
Another one used to have very
        long hair.
They all showed me
how much pain I can take,
how much love I deserve.

call me
the princess
of whippits

call me
angel
mother fucker

Marianne Agnes

Favorite energy drink: water

Favorite fast food: cancel me but probably chick fil a. you can take the girl out of the south but you cant take the south out of the girl

After Supper

after supper
you hunt me like a dog
dragging myself to you pathetic,
I beg for your sneer,
drool for those sharp fingers
your barbed tongue

you peel me apart
scrupulously
not letting a drop go to waste

strung high a skinned doe,
you clean your knife and watch over me
and I exhale into ether

Maurane

Song stuck in your head: I'm like a bird from Nelly Furtado has been stuck in my head for the last 10 years

Favorite film: Wild at heart, Fallen angels and Irreversible are my top 3.

Random fact about you: I was conceived through sperm donation

I'M WRITING ABOUT MY DEAD FRIEND BECAUSE THERAPY IS FUCKING EXPENSIVE

Me and Benjamin had a lot in common
One of them was our desire to suck Louis
Big round cheeks
Dark brown hair
Luscious pink lips

we wanted to suck Louis so badly
that we were ready to forget that we had no attraction
for each other
to suck him together

I'm sure Louis' dick
Is small but good licking
smells like rose soap
And is pink like his lips

Louis didn't know we both fantasized about his dick
In fact we both never really spoke to him
It was our thing, our sharing dream, not his

now that Benjamin is dead
I don't want to suck Louis's dick so much anymore
I would stop sucking dicks to bring him back to life
I would suck the ugliest dick on earth to bring him back
to life

Maya Osep
Height: 5'4
Hair color: Poopy poop brown
Favorite fictional character: Spongeboob
Most expensive purchase: Fugly $900 Off-White jacket at a boutique in Mykonos
Where is your favorite place on Earth?: El Prado !
Last text you received: "Please never contact me again"
How would you like to die?: In as much pain as possible

Happy Birthday Mr. President

It was two weeks before Coachella weekend. My failed musician boyfriend was DJing a destination birthday in Palm Springs for a group of geriatrics and their respective escorts. The birthday boy was literally named Michael Scott and it was the big four-oh. We signed NDAs upon entering the illustrious compound.

We met the other peasants working the event (besides my then boyfriend and his DJ partner). I noticed "dancers" making their way in. I suppose it was fitting; it was his 40th birthday after all! He had no choice but to pull out all the stops.

The men and their arm candy were all decked out in white clothes. Something about a white party always seemed so sinister to me; like, what are you, a eugenicist? Would you call me a mulatto unironically?

The old codgers and their floozies filed into the pool area. To refer to it as the "pool area" would be an understatement; it looked like a man-made lake or a backdrop from the Truman Show. At one point in the night, a guest jumped out of a helicopter into said pool.

I felt deeply out of place. I was the only whore at this party fucking for free. But I couldn't help but notice a familiar face. It was the FATHER to two of the biggest supermodels in the world; Bella and Gigi's dad, Mohamed Hadid. I couldn't believe my eyes. These were definitely high rollers.

The night went on and I got obliterated. I abused the hell out of the open bar built into the pool which resembled the Taj Mahal. I was bored and trying to occupy myself while my boyfriend and his degenerate friend played shitty house music. I shuffled inside the main house and ran into the estate's indentured servants. I could feel their judgement, but they were used to this. I'm sure they assumed I was part of the herd of escorts — or maybe I stuck out like a sore thumb.

The girls looked like Fashion Nova models who went on "sponsored trips" with Saudi billionaires to "model;" the types that Leo DiCaprio would fuck with headphones on. I would never be one of those girls. Leo would spit in my face if I even tried. His bodyguards would shoot me dead right there. "Don't get near him you bitch!"

I stumbled my way into the bathroom and noticed a significant amount of blood on the floor. I thought I was seeing things and decided to ignore it. The nice people at the estate would handle it. This is what NDAs are for, I told myself.

I got on the swing to pass the time; not that kind. One of the lovely guests pulled the swing back so far I thought I was going to fly off into the pavement and crack my head open. I'm sure it wouldn't be the first body they'd have had to bury.

I decided to take a nap on some patio furniture when I was suddenly awakened by a mad man. My boyfriend thought I'd run off with one of the old codgers and got irate. Who did he think I was?

Two weeks later, we returned to the same house and ran into his ex; some broad who had a restraining order against him. She was going around the valley telling people I was a drug addict...weird. We flew out of the party and into an Uber.

I could barely breathe from the meth-laced coke and stuck my head out the window like a dog. I prayed to L. Ron to absolve me of my sins and to grant me another day. So much for that NDA...

I COULDN'T TELL
IF YOU WERE
SERIOUS / WHEN
YOU TOLD ME TO
POP MY PUSSY /
BUT I STILL
POPPED MY PUSSY

I DO SIT-UPS
AND PRACTICE
KARATE / CUZ I
WANNA BE
READY / FOR
VIOLENCE

Meat Stevens

Where is your favorite place on Earth?: Camp Wayne For Boys
in Preston Park Pennsylvania
Favorite fictional character: Stone Cold Steve Austin
Best kiss: Siena Foster-Soltis
Last Halloween costume: Stone Cold Steve Austin
Favorite axe body spray: Phoenix.

Nude Beach

Nude beach
Waves crashing
Smoking cigs
Modelo Micheladas
Dick sucked to Leon Redbone on cassette
Diddy Wa Diddie
Double time
Watching pelicans dive
No one passing by
Once dick is being sucked
people start to come
What do you want to do?
I want to fuck you and write about it
That's what the publishers want she says
Would be nice
A pool of precum collects in my hole and boils in the sun
I press the tip of my cock to my thigh
We watch the strings pull and break
She tongues it up and laughs
Shine on, Shine on Harvest Moon

medb

Have you ever stolen anything?: Maybelline New York eyeliner from Tesco and a Princess Diana pocket mirror from a Camden tourist trap store

Worst breakup: 28 year old Virgo with an opera gloves fetish, dumped me in the parking lot of an allotments and tried to use his aunt dying as an excuse

Most embarrassing moment: every time I've been dumped by a man who has never left home

Ode to the N109

we were all dancing around outside the
Moon Under Water
drunk in Dulwich
downtown suburban
sexy depressive
on the edge of the city lights no one can touch you
and it was October just like I remember it
then the foxes came out and started fucking
and we got on the bus and stayed on it forever

Nestan Nikouradze
Zodiac sign: scorpio
Secret talent: i can cast spells
Favorite actor: winona ryder
Favorite candy: ferrero rocher

Kangaroo

Gift me a kangaroo please
a baby one with grey-blue eyes
it should sit on a round tea-table
and sip chamomile with silver spoons
Lick the porcelain
make me sway
Tiny tongue touch marble
carry me away

Deer

I try my best to make the legs that support me
look like sticks.
They click like hooves on the cement.
I stand on shoes with heels like twigs.
I keep my calluses smooth and my skin
fresh.
My torso is adorned with fur that puffs up in the wind.
I tilt my head and place one hand on my collar
when lighting my cigarette.

s m van de kamp
Three favorite colors: Jade green, cobalt blue, HEX b36161
Believe in luck?: I believe in privilege..
Believe in love at first sight?: No, sorry.

Untitled

you are my
oh no not again
and my
yes yes please

God's Dreamhouse Floor

god's dreamhouse floor
must be littered
with a lot of light, a lot of
expensive skincare products
and $500 earrings
strewn with uber black drivers
in nervous performance
with a germaphobe
here on earth i'm so tired
i can't work
instead i deepclean the bathroom
in penance or purgatory
scrub away piss and
little black hairs from the toilet
only to puke in it the next day
too many tequila shots
is the morning after ever holy?
at least the bowl was clean
sit on my face fuck me
wait what happened
last night?
what is on the floor?
on splintered wood sits
the headless pigeon
i put on the curb last week
a small scratch from a cat,
that murderess, and my tight voice
i'm dead for the day but tomorrow
i'll be alive

Sarah Elda
Most expensive purchase: The 6 hour taxi ride that I had to take in order to get my cat from Paris to London

Baby

Baby tell the nurse that the baby is coming
and I don't have the nursery ready,
I don't have a name picked out
and I don't want to know the sex
and I don't want to know the baby
because it doesn't know me like that

baby tell the baby I don't love you
and we're too young and we don't know what a baby is
baby tell the birthing pool we could only fill it half way be-
cause
last month's water bill was out of control and it was your
fault,
what kind of grown man takes baths every night

and baby, tell me baby,
what kind of baby would you like, because
maybe if I can, I can will myself to give you what you want
if that's a baby you want baby, I can make a baby for you
baby
to make you love me like you'd love my baby
but baby don't call the baby your baby

baby
will you ask my baby why it destroyed me, baby?
why my stomach's loose, why I don't bleed like before
baby?
but my baby is my baby, baby
you can't help my baby like I can baby
I grow and make my baby grow with my body baby
the baby needs me more than you baby
tell the doctor it's his baby,
that the baby will see him before it sees anyone
it's not my baby and it's not your baby, baby

Toilet/Coke

and it was porcelain plastic
and it was placid pools of plumbing
and it was a thought of an impulse dispersed,
where again humiliation is forever
and so is that foot of metal
I kneeled over in distraction and broke skin
and thought I'd remember this too
even if it hadn't etched itself into my calf,
there would've been recognition
and it was a vial and then plastic again,
plastic always finds its way into memory
and it was the thought of a thought occuring
and the check and the in
there was humiliation there too:
when I thought I could take as I had taken before
it saddened me to learn that I had ever only taken
and what I took I didn't have any use for,
and what I took I had taken before,
and what I could take I wouldn't feel,
now that I must only fill

summer has great graphics
smells like cum and sunscreen

Sarah Velk

Worst breakup: not giving him the satisfaction

Most embarrassing moment: i don't get embarrassed i get awe-
some

Drake vs. Kendrick?: DRIZZY DRAKE 4 LIFE THEY COULD
NEVER MAKE ME HATE YOU BABY!!!!!

Best kiss: skateboarders

Actually Really Smart

crows sit high in a barren tree
surveying *la terre gris*
if they had teeth they'd chomp at us
and they'd laugh when we jumped

if the birds can sing then so can i.
if you can be mean then i'll be a terrorist.
if the dirt road corrupts the air with dust
we'll wait for the rain.

Siena Foster-Soltis
Height: 5'6"
Zodiac sign: Taurus
Last time you cried: Today
Secret talent: I can pull a small spoon out of my nose
Believe in luck?: Yes.
Believe in love at first sight?: No.
Tattoos: None.

Metzgerhund

She ordered the least potent thing she could find on the menu - the most neutral - the least information.

That's all you want?

That's perfect.

Is that going to be enough?

I'll get two then.

He ordered a pastrami sandwich, onion rings and a Pabst blue ribbon.

She thought that was inconsiderate.

It was, at best, careless.

At its worst, his order was pathetic.

So this was his true self? The sweat of overcooked onions and sweet vinegar?

It's not like she expected much more, but she forced a smile and sipped her vodka soda and pretended like she had to run pee.

She bumped into their waitress on the way to the bathroom.

Her breasts were hard.

Her face was frozen.

So sorry about that.

Oh, I'm so sorry.

She locked the stall door and pulled out her phone: I ac-
tually do want to go out tonight. I'm not busy anymore.

She waited for a response - a way out of the evening, but
received nothing.

She flushed the empty toilet and washed her hands.

When she returned to her seat, he asked her if she had
any siblings.

I have one brother.

Oh, I have two.

Are you close?

We weren't when we were younger, but now we talk
sometimes.

Me too.

The waitress with the ossified breasts and mulish face
set her plate down in front of her.

Two white chicken breasts.

No sauce.

He asked for extra sauce and the waitress left.

He asked her if she wanted a bite of his sandwich.

She politely declined.

She checked her phone under the table.

Still nothing.

A large man with thinning hair and a mohair suit jacket

entered the restaurant and stood by the door.

She didn't know what compelled her to look up from her phone, but she did.

His face was red and his mouth was runtish.

He gripped a short black rope.

Her eyes followed its trail down to the floor where a wide-legged rottweiler stood panting in the doorframe.

The dog's body moved with each breath.

His stomach would swell, sucking in air and compress when exhaling.

He was meat and pure muscle with legs thick and con-toured.

The sides of his body pulsated with each step he took.

It seemed like he could have been smiling.

The waitress sat the man and his dog at the table closest to the door.

The man sat, but the dog continued to stand.

He panted heavily.

You could hear him breathing from across the room.

He looked at her.

She noticed the dog's penis and then quickly turned away.

Who brings their dog into a restaurant? He asked half jokingly.

His voice faded, drowned by the sound of the dog's hungry gasps for air.

It was all she could hear.

Maybe he has a disability? I shouldn't judge.

She said nothing.

You're insanely pretty by the way.

What?

You're really pretty.

She looked up again at the dog.

He hadn't moved.

He could've just been facing in her general direction, though she felt as if she was being watched.

Oh, thank you.

Yeah.

There was silence.

She delicately cut off a slice of chicken, skewered it with her fork, and placed it softly in between her lips.

What's your brother like?

He's older.

Her eyes darted around the room.

She tried to stare at the man across from her, but she kept wandering.

How much older?

He used to play sports, but now he works for Amtrak.

Railroads, right?

Uh, yeah.

She felt around in her bag for her phone.

The dog's eyes followed her hands.

He's older, six years older.

That's kinda a big age gap.

Yeah.

She felt the palm of her hand on the back of her phone case.

She pulled it up from her bag and held it out in front of her.

I'm sorry, I really need to head out.

Oh, already?

Yeah my friend just went through a breakup, she needs me right now.

Oh.

I'm sorry to run out on you so suddenly.

It's okay.

I can pay for the meal.

Don't worry about it.

Are you sure?

It's fine. Don't worry.

She stood up, already slipping on her coat.

I hate to run out on you, she just really needs me.

You don't have to explain yourself. I said it was fine.

She gathered herself and picked up her bag.

I'll see you, okay? She grimaced.

She headed towards the door.

She was leaving.

She locked her eyes on the outside.

She could see her car parked across the street.

That was where she was going.

She was going to walk to her car and drive home or drive
to the bar or to her friend's or anywhere that wasn't here.

She suddenly felt a rush of warmth.

It spread down her body, down her spine, into her stom-
ach. It consumed her.

Her arms went numb.

Her legs floated above the ground. Her feet detached
themselves from her ankles.

Her chest expanded, exploded.

She stared at the ceiling.

She could only see out of one eye.

She was lying face up.

She was scattered across the restaurant floor.

She looked into the eyes of the dog, now hovering over her.

He breathed into her.

She heard people in the background. She heard the man. The waitress. Her date.

But she only saw the dog.

She only felt the dog.

Her blood in him, his breath in her.

one day we'll all be MILFS
we'll sit topless in the backyard
flirt w/ the highschool boys
take a sip of white wine
and say "fuck wasn't it awful?
being young and pretty?

Sofia Hoefig
Zodiac sign: scorpio
Hair color: fake blonde
Most expensive purchase: my balenciaga handbag <3
Most embarrassing moment: like last week when two kids said
"ew she's taking a picture of a dead bird" cause i was taking a
picture of a dead bird...

Ode to the Autistic Girls Who Look Like Courtney Love

dark roots outgrown
on uneven toned hair
shades of blonde in yellow,
white
purple

swollen lipped and sullen eyed
all of your doll parts.
your lipstick bleeds across your whole face
we all know you are drunk

you cannot mask it
could you ever mask it?

Sophia Georghiou
Zodiac sign: Cancer
Three favorite colors: Basil green, lilac, tomato
What do you want to be when you grow up?: A ballerina

Now Hiring: The Other Woman, Part-Time

Near the end of my final shift,
he sent everyone else home early,
watched as I slapped a mop
against the cheeks of the kitchen,
chucked the tables together
like pulled teeth, cheshire-cat-smiling.
I was so angry he was married,
behind the counter, between the coffee
and walnut cake, the curdled abortion
of last season's milkshakes.
Even on his way to the storage cupboard
I followed with an air of vengeance
circling my head
like a chaotic halo, the light he
would soon snuff, fucking
me, exhausted-puff, against the empty shelves.

Stephanie Yue Duhem
Last beverage: Spindrift strawberry lemonade
Last Halloween costume: Dana Scully

flying saucer

a still
but still gleaming
eye
very much alive

was the moon
that night

over whose
avaricious surface
a dark disc

darkened

like a coin laid
on an eye-
lid

i
turned to my friend
a blonde as blonde
as a blonde
in a movie
poster said

did you see that??

but her mouth
was an o

as in u.f.o.
object-
ing to the sight
above

i didn't tell her what
i thought

which was that
you
had sent the saucer
since
our earthly love
had faltered
and
you still wanted me

to have a ride

yes love so i see
you will do anything!!

and love yes
i am beaming
 up

up to go anywhere!!

as your bride...

ZELDA⁶⁴

i wanna be
the thingy
floating
in a dungeon
that u run into
to refill all ur
heart containers

Swan Scissors
Last beverage you drank: cherry juicy juicy
Secret talent: peeing on weak men
Song stuck in your head: blue (ba da dee)

3 Poems

I want to smoke a
tea joint — the
kind Grace told me
about. I want to ride
horses & dick all through
the night.

a space to rip a
part
bleed into   a
space   to
drip wax into
the cracks &
carve poems in
to   the wood
floors ,

I was really scared to
I was really scared
to touch
to touch to
let myself be
touched I was
scared I was
pretty scared
 yea I
  yea.
   but
 it was good . nice yea
it was sweet
 so soft so
 very gentle
  it was easier
  than I thought

it was better
than I thought
 yea . it was
   pretty beautiful
    to touch & to be touched
    it was like crystal .
      to be healed
        to heal
         to be healed to

████@hotmail.com